For my brother, Tim - *H.O.*
For Alastair - *M.R.*

MYRIAD BOOKS LIMITED
35 Bishopsthorpe Road, London SE26 4PA

First published in 1999 by
FRANCES LINCOLN LIMITED
4 Torriano Mews
Torriano Avenue
London NW5 2RZ

Little Brother and the Cough copyright © Frances Lincoln 1999
Text copyright © Hiawyn Oram 1999
Illustrations copyright © Mary Rees 1999

Hiawyn Oram and Mary Rees have asserted their right to be identified as
the author and illustrator of this work in accordance with the Copyright, Designs and Patents Act, 1988.

ISBN 1 84746 045 3
EAN 9 781 84746 045 5

Printed in China

Little Brother
and the COUGH

Hiawyn Oram

Illustrated by Mary Rees

MYRIAD BOOKS LIMITED

The day my mother went away and came back
with a baby, I got a cough.

"COUGH!" went the Cough.

"Come and say hello to your little brother,"
they said.

"NO!" coughed the Cough. "WON'T," coughed the Cough. "COUGH! COUGH! COUGH!"

"Hush, ssh, your little brother is sleeping,"
they said.

"AND WE ARE COUGHING!" coughed the Cough.
"A BIG NOISY COUGH!"

My little brother was fed at all hours.
"Come and watch your little brother being fed," they said.

"NO!" coughed the Cough. "We're watching television now and forever."

My little brother was bathed in his own bath with
his own soap and his own shampoo, even though
he hardly had a hair on his head.
"Come and see your little brother splashing," they said.

"WHY?" went the Cough. "We know what splashing is. SPLASHING IS SPLASHING!"

My little brother was given rattles and
cuddly toys and a musical rolling ball.

"NAAAUGH!" coughed the Cough.
"WE WANT RATTLES AND CUDDLY TOYS
AND A BABY'S ROLLING BALL!"

My little brother smiled his first smile and everyone
in the neighbourhood was called in to see.
"Isn't this great? Isn't this sweet?" they cooed.
"Your little brother can smile!"

"AND WE CAN STAND ON OUR HEAD,"
coughed the Cough.

My little brother was put in his pram under the tree.
"Let's creep up to him," coughed the Cough.
"No one is watching. Let's rock his pram…

AND ROCK HIS PRAM AND ROCK HIS PRAM
AND ROCK HIS PRAM UNTIL IT TIPS OVER
AND TIPS HIM OUT!" coughed the Cough…

And this time everybody heard and came running.
"What a Bad Cough you have!" they cried.
"What a very Bad Cough. What a very very VERY
Bad Cough…"

And they put us to bed and gave us hot drinks
and hot water bottles and a cuddly bear and
some colouring books and a musical box with
a ballerina inside…

and sat on the bed and soothed us and read
to us and coloured in with us until the Cough
decided it had no more to do in our house and
crept away in the night…

and I could get up and say, "Hello,
Little Brother… This is a musical box.
And I am your Big Sister…"

and watch him…

watch him…

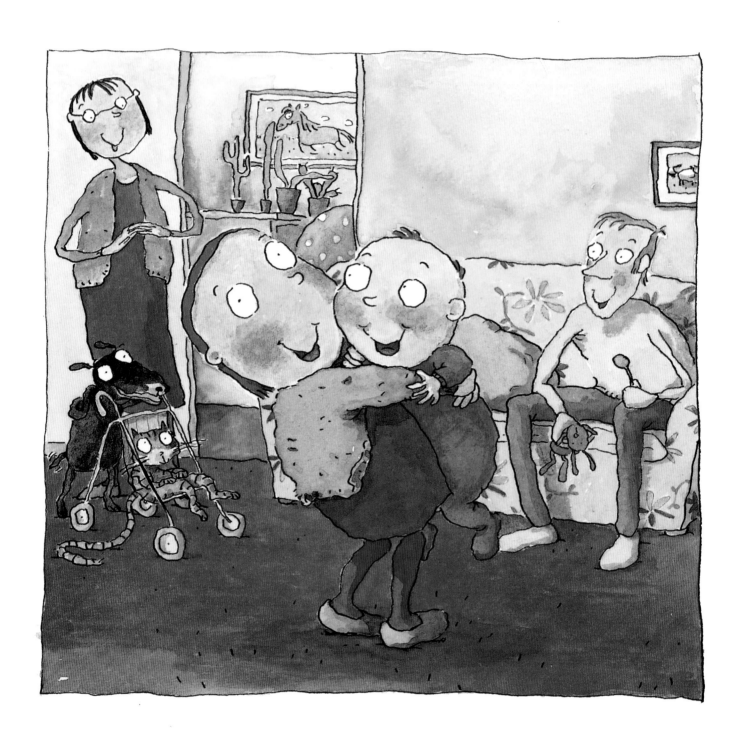

SMILE!